The Official
ELMORE JUNIOR HIGH SCHOOL
YEARBOOK

PSS!
PRICE STERN SLOAN
An Imprint of Penguin Group (USA) LLC

PRICE STERN SLOAN
Published by the Penguin Group
Penguin Group (USA) LLC, 375 Hudson Street, New York, New York 10014, USA

USA | Canada | UK | Ireland | Australia | New Zealand | India | South Africa | China

penguin.com
A Penguin Random House Company

Written by Jake Black

™ and © Turner Broadcasting System Europe Limited, Cartoon Network (s14)

Published in 2014 by Price Stern Sloan, a division of Penguin Young Readers Group, 345 Hudson Street, New York, New York 10014. *PSS!* is a registered trademark of Penguin Group (USA) LLC. Manufactured in China.

ISBN 978-0-8431-8049-7   10 9 8 7 6 5 4 3 2 1

INTRODUCTION
by Principal Brown

Students, teachers, and Miss Simian, this was another fantastic year at Elmore Junior High. Everyone had a great time. Oh, the memories! This yearbook should help you remember those memories for as long as you can remember them. I hope you never forget your time at Elmore Junior High! Make sure you get all your friends to sign your yearbook.

And we'll see you next year!

TABLE OF CONTENTS

Principal Brown

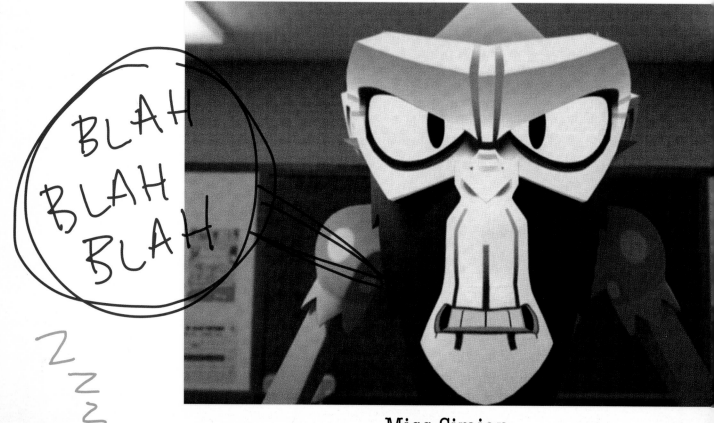

Miss Simian

Rocky Robinson

Mr. Small

The Librarian

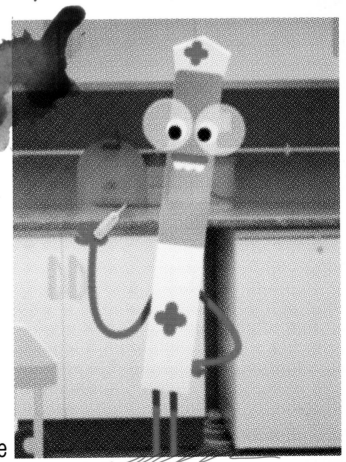

The Nurse

STUDENT PORTRAITS

Alan

Anais Watterson

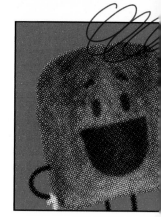

Anton

Banana Joe

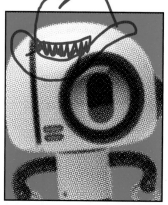

Bobert

Carmen

Carrie

Clayton

Darwin Watterson

Dog

Dolly

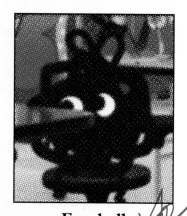

Fuzzball

The Green Bear

Gumball Watterson

Hector

Hot Dog Guy

Idaho

Jamie

Juke

Leslie

Masami

Molly Collins

Mushroom

Ocho

Penny Fitzgerald

Rob

Sussie

Teri

Tina Rex

Tobias Wilson

William

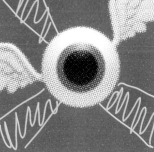

CLUBS

After-school clubs are great! You can make a lot of friends in a club, and you can do a lot of really fun stuff! At Elmore Junior High, we have several clubs, including:

ANGER MANAGEMENT CLUB

REJECT CLUB

DRAMA CLUB

SOCCER CLUB

COMPUTER CLUB

SYNCHRONIZED-SWIMMING CLUB

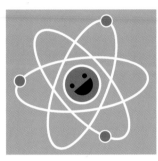

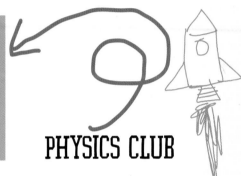

PHYSICS CLUB

In the space provided, list the clubs you want to join. If your club isn't on the list here, create one! It can be a club about anything!

FIELD TRIP

It's great to get away from school for a little while to go on a field trip. You can learn something new in an exciting way when you're out in the world! These are some of our favorite moments from this year's field trip—the picnic in the forest!

Remember to stay with the group and always listen to the teacher. If you do get lost or separated, don't panic. Ask an adult to help you find your school group.

I GUESS WE DIDN'T FOLLOW THOSE RULES WHEN WE WENT ON OUR TRIP TO THE WOODS.

SCHOOL DANCES

Bust a move! Elmore Junior High is known all over the world for its epic school dances. I mean, c'mon, it's home to the banana dance and GUMBALL style! Maybe you don't think you can dance. But you can! You just got to get out on the dance floor and move! Even grouchy Mr. Robinson loves to dance!

I wanna sing!

I wanna dance!

I wanna touch the sky

 with my own two

 hands!

If I sing to the world,

 it'll set me free,

 and let me be who I

 wanna be!

Dance, dance and sing!

 I'm gonna give it my

 everything!

And fortune and

 fame will be at my

 command,

As I whisk you off to a

 wonderland!

I'll hip-hop and jive with my heart and my soul!

I'll press down to the bump, to the rock and the roll,

I'll tango and jango, and the hanky and panky. I'll fly like a
bird if you set me free!

Like a skylark on the wing, or a rosebud in the spring,

Like a gangster and his bling, like fish bait from a sling,

Like a puppet with no string, like an English feudal king!

Like all those kinds of wonderful, wonderful things!

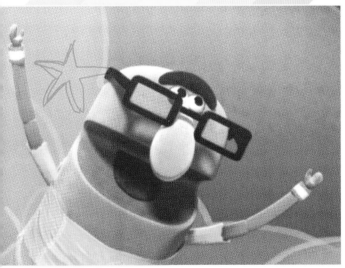

I wanna be freeeeeeeee!

SCHOOL SPIRIT

School spirit is a wonderful thing! It's what makes us cheer for our sports teams. It helps us take care of the school, and it's what helps us always remember the good times we had while attending Elmore Junior High!

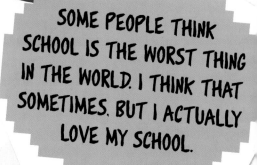

SOME PEOPLE THINK SCHOOL IS THE WORST THING IN THE WORLD. I THINK THAT SOMETIMES, BUT I ACTUALLY LOVE MY SCHOOL.

TIME CAPSULE

Our school and our town have been around for a long time. Check out these pictures that we found when we came across the school's time capsule. Everything looks pretty much the same, but older, because it's all in black-and-white.

THE ART DEPARTMENT

Art is a great form of expression. You can create art to describe how you feel about anything. The Art Department at Elmore Junior High will help you bring out your artistic side. Just look at these paintings by the super-talented Watterson family! On the next page, create your own masterpiece. You can use pencils, crayons, paint, clay . . . whatever you want! Just express yourself!

oh yeah!!

VOLUNTEERING

One aspect of school is learning how to be a good citizen and make a positive contribution to your community. These Elmore Junior High students have made volunteering a big part of their lives, helping to give back to their neighborhoods and communities.

They volunteered by helping an older neighbor do a lot of chores around his house. They cleaned his house and tidied his yard, making the area look more beautiful. They even helped him with his car!

SCIENCE

Everything always comes back to science. Everything in the universe works because of science. You can learn about science at our school, Elmore Junior High, in the science lab! Be careful with the experiments you try. You don't want to blow up an ant farm and be attacked by millions of angry, homeless ants!

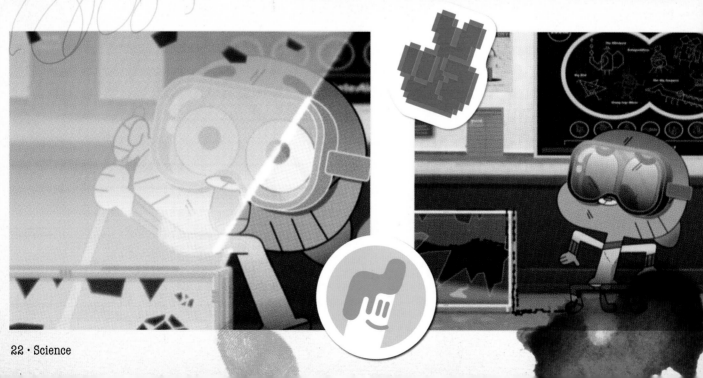

ENGLISH

Reading and writing are important skills to learn in school. They will help you when you are a grown-up out in the real world, but you probably already knew that because you're reading the words and captions in your yearbook. (Unless you're not, and just looking at the pictures . . . but you're not doing that because you're reading this right now.) If you can read, thank a teacher.

SPORTS

Elmore Junior High School is known throughout the area as being a great place for sports. Sports teach students to be their best, and to work hard. They also teach good sportsmanship and focus. There are all kinds of sports out there to play. Soccer is especially popular here at Elmore Junior High, but racquetball, tennis, basketball, karate, swimming, and many others are also popular. What are your favorite sports?

CHEERLEADING

No sports event is complete without cheerleaders leading the crowd in some great cheers. Cheerleaders help the players feel more determined to win. Let's hear it for the cheer squad! Hip-hip hooray!

SOCCER GAME

You can play soccer just like your EJHS friends! All you need is two quarters and a penny. You and a friend each take a quarter and slide it across the page, bumping the penny toward your goal.
Whoever bumps the penny into the goal the most times in five minutes wins!

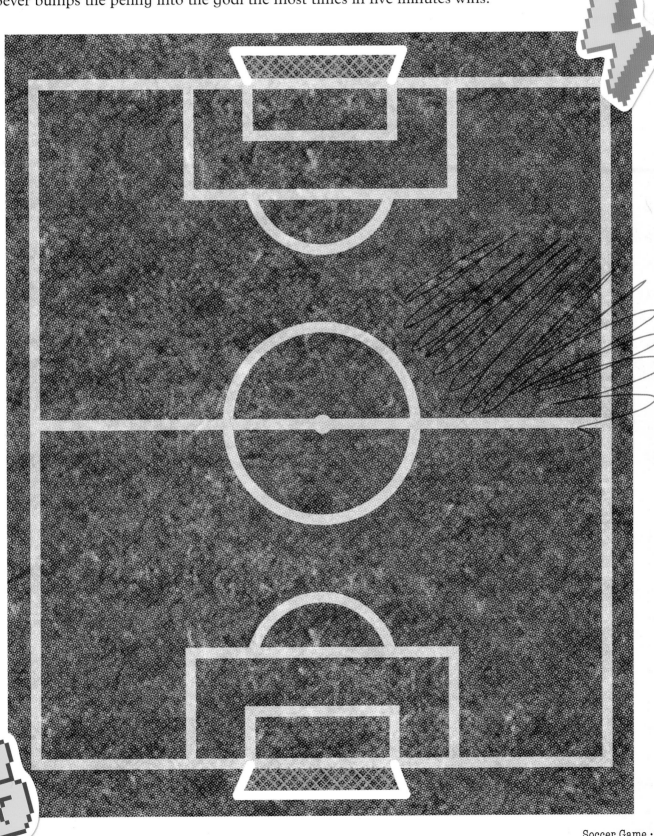

MOVIES

Everyone loves to relax by watching a great movie. You can rent them from the video store, watch them on TV, or even download them (legally) online. Elmore Junior High students voted, and the most popular movie this year was *Alligators on a Train*.

What are your favorite movies? Write them out in the space provided.

FOOD

Lunchtime! It's one of the best times of the day! You get to eat nutritious meals from the school cafeteria, and hang out with your friends. Elmore Junior High's cafeteria is awesome. The food is so good!

DARWIN AND I LOVE HAVING LUNCH IN THE CAFETERIA. YOU CAN ALWAYS COUNT ON SOME LUNCHTIME DRAMA!

The cafeteria is always looking for food suggestions from the students. In the space below, write out what foods you want the cafeteria to make in the future.

HOW I SPENT MY SUMMER VACATION

Summer vacation is the best! Elmore Junior High School students really know how to live it up! Whether playing sports with friends, renting a movie, helping around the house, camping, having food fights, or whatever, having fun over the summer is really the greatest thing in the whole world. Here are several summer memories and pictures from EJHS students!

FEATURED STUDENT

Congratulations! You are this year's featured student in the Elmore Junior High School yearbook! Tell us a little about yourself, and be sure to draw or paste a picture of yourself in the space provided on the next page.

Name:

Which country and city do you live in?

What is your best subject at school?

Stick a picture of yourself here.

How many brothers and sisters do you have?

What do you want to be when you grow up?

What school clubs do you belong to?

AROUND TOWN

Living in Elmore is awesome. Epic. There's so much to do in this town, it's amazing. You can go to the museum, the mall, or the junkyard. Here are some of Elmore Junior High students' favorite hangout spots and places to visit in Elmore. Write your favorite memories of each place in the space provided beneath the picture.

FASHION

What's the hottest fashion in the halls of Elmore Junior High?

Not this:

Here we see Gumball Watterson modeling his stylish brown sweater.

Darwin Watterson's got some pretty kickin' kicks.

Tobias Wilson shows off the latest in athletic gear.

Jamie's got amazing hair.

Tina Rex really knows how to show off a toothy smile.

No one looks sleeker than Bobert.

Principal Brown has got the best eyeglasses we've ever seen.

Dolly is cooler than ice.

MUSIC

Music is a huge deal around Elmore Junior High School. It seems like everyone sings all the time. But maybe the most memorable song around EJHS was when Mr. Small, our fearless guidance counselor, dressed up like the Honesty Bear and laid down the beats and rhymes with "The Honesty Rap."

Uh-uh-uh-uh Honesty!
(crab scratch) **Honesty!**
Break it down,

When you wanna be honest, just beware!
The truth hurts in this nitrogenic atmosphere!

You gotta wake up, realize and recognize!
Sometimes the truth has strategical lies!

But keep them lies of a manageable size,
Or tears will arise, and hurt their eyes!

So before you speak, it's best to remember:
(spoken very quickly) **Each individual**
case will require a specific
judgment call depending on who you are
talking to and the context of the conversation!

Was music your favorite subject? Show your musical skills by writing a new song on this composition paper!

SCHOOL MAP

These places should be totally familiar to you by now! The halls lined with lockers. The cafeteria. The classrooms. The gym. These are the places that we've called home...er...*school* for the last year. Where was your favorite place in the school? Did you ever get lost? On the next page, show your knowledge of the school grounds by completing the Elmore Junior High map maze!

START ENGLISH CLASS

MR. SMALL'S OFFICE

LIBRARY

PRINCIPAL'S OFFICE

CAFETERIA

SCIENCE CLASS

TRACK

GYM

LOCKERS

LOCKER ROOM

SWIMMING POOL

PLAYGROUND

FINISH

SCHOOL LIFE

Oh, school. The place where we spend at least six and a half hours a day, five days per week. It's almost like we live here. As long as we're stuck here, we might as well make the most of it. These pics show some of the best moments from the last year. Do you remember when . . .

PARTIES!

Everyone loves to *par-tay* down, right? School parties are okay, but what're really awesome are house parties. You never know what craziness will happen if you go to a house party. Sometimes you need to bring a date, but mostly it's all about going to the party, hanging out, dancing, eating, and, well, partying!

A DAY IN THE LIFE

What is your typical day like? For seventh-grader Gumball Watterson,
it looks something like this:

Get up

Eat breakfast

Go to school

Hang out with friends

Go home

Eat dinner

Play video games

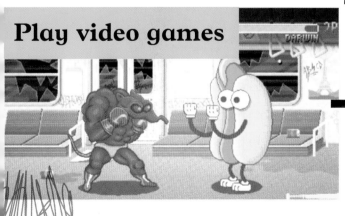

Go to bed

HALLOWEEN

Holidays are always fun around Elmore Junior High. Halloween is especially fun. Who doesn't love to dress up and scare your friends? Plus, think of the candy. All that glorious candy. For this past Halloween, several Elmore students visited a haunted house. It was a wild night full of fear and fun.

CHRISTMAS

Christmastime is a wonderful season. It's about love, joy, and kindness. Every year, EJHS students eagerly await Santa Claus's arrival—and look forward to receiving the presents he brings. They all want to be on Santa's good list, of course. However, it's important to remember that it's better to give than receive, even with Santa.

FUTURE GOALS

We go to school so we can create great lives for ourselves. Another part of that is setting goals for the future. What are your goals? Write them down in the space provided.

OUR FAVORITE THINGS

We all know that *Alligators on a Train* is pretty much everyone at Elmore Junior High's favorite movie of all time. What are some other things you like? Write your answers to the questions below, and tell the world about your favorite things!

Favorite TV Show:
....

Favorite Movie:
....

Favorite Color:
....

Favorite Book:
....

Favorite Food:
....

Favorite Song:
....

Favorite Music Group:
....

Favorite Place to Hang Out:
....

Favorite Flavor of Ice Cream:
....

Favorite Fruit:
....

MOST LIKELY TO . . .

One of the things yearbooks are known for is predicting the futures of students. Check out our predictions for students here at EJHS.

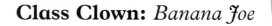

Class Clown: *Banana Joe*

Most Likely to Save the World: *Darwin Watterson*

Most Likely to Be MVP of the Big Game: *Tobias Wilson*

Most Likely to Join a Demolition Derby: *Tina Rex*

Most Likely to Be a Therapist: *Leslie*

Most Likely to Be a Pilot: *Alan*

Most Likely to Be an Astronaut: *Bobert*

Most Likely to Be a Nurse: *Teri*

Most Likely to Be a Millionaire: *Masami*

Most Likely to Be a Rock Star: *Juke*

BEHIND THE SCENES OF THE YEARBOOK

Ever wonder what goes on behind the scenes at the yearbook? There's a lot that needs to be done to make the yearbook as good as it can be every year. We have to take a ton of pictures (as you've seen in this edition of the yearbook), write the captions and the words at the top of the page (like these words right here), and, well, that's pretty much it. But a lot of students get freaked out about having their yearbook picture taken, like Gumball Watterson. Check out everything he went through to get his photo just right!

PARENT DEDICATIONS

GUMBALL, WE'RE SO PROUD OF EVERYTHING YOU'VE DONE THIS YEAR. YOU'RE THE GREATEST SON ANYONE COULD EVER ASK FOR! WE LOVE YOU!
—*Mom and Dad*

DARWIN, EVER SINCE YOU GREW LEGS AND BECAME A MEMBER OF OUR FAMILY, WE'VE BEEN SO GLAD TO HAVE YOU AROUND. CONGRATULATIONS ON EVERYTHING YOU DID THIS YEAR.
—*Mom and Dad*

Tina, you really showed them this year, Kiddo! Way to go!
—Dad

Tobias:
Roses are red,
violets are blue,
sports are fun,
and so are you!
—Mom and Dad

Penny, I'm proud to be your dad!
—Dad

AUTOGRAPHS

Collect as many autographs from your friends as you can on these pages!

Have a great
summer!—Gumball

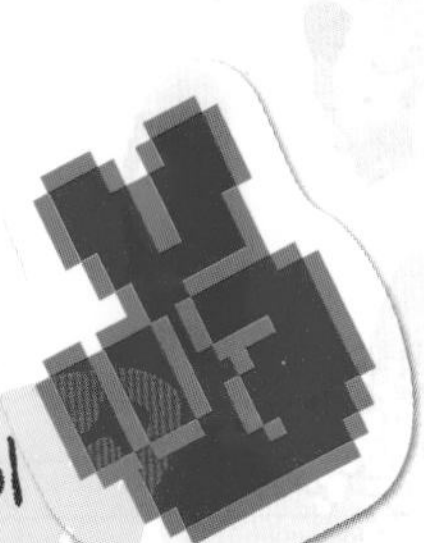

UR 2 Cool
2 Be 4-gotten
—Penny

See ya next year!
—Tina

Don't take rocks for granite!
  –Principal Brown

I'm so glad we're friends!—Darwin

Thanks for all
your hard work
in class
—Miss Simian

Later, tater!—Idaho

This year
rocked!
—Ocho

Call me! We'll hang out
this summer!—Sussie

Don't forget me!-Rob

STAY COOL!-
DOLLY

DON'T EVER CHANGE!-CLAYTON